ELLI WO
Swashbuckle Lil
The Secret Pirate
ILLUSTRATED BY LAURA ELLEN ANDERSON
MACMILLAN CHILDRENS BOOKS

First published 2016 by Macmillan Children's Books
an imprint of Pan Macmillan
20 New Wharf Road, London N1 9RR
Associated companies throughout the world
www.panmacmillan.com

ISBN 978-1-5098-0882-3

1 3 5 7 9 8 6 4 2

A CIP catalogue record for this book is available from the British Library.

Printed and bound by CPI Group (UK) Ltd, Croydon CR0 4YY

To Thomas and Oscar
E.W.

For Gill and Matt –
fellow partners in crime
and coffee consumption!
L.E.A

The Secret Pirate

1

When Lil sat at school doing spellings and sums,

Nobody, nobody guessed

That she wasn't at all like an ordinary girl,

And that under her jumper and vest . . .

Lil was a pirate, a swashbuckling pirate,

Whose home was a ship with great sails,

Who had travelled the seas in the blustery breeze

And had ridden the waves with huge whales.

At weekends Lil never sat watching TV,

Or played on the swings in the park,

But instead she might fight with a monster all night

In waters that shimmered with sharks.

No, nobody guessed at Lil's pirating life,

Though the children all thought it quite odd

That instead of school dinners Lil went to the pond . . .

And tried to catch haddock and cod.

And that noise from Lil's schoolbag –

what could it be?

A shuffle? A rustle? A squawk?

But maybe Lil's friends had imagined it all;

Bags, after all, couldn't *talk*!

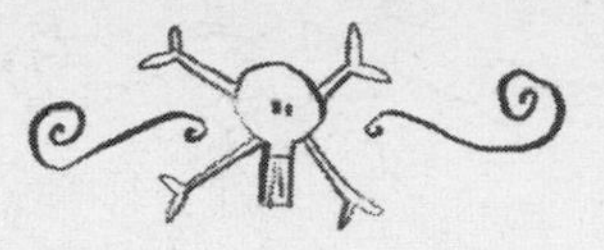

Sometimes Lil simply forgot where she was
As she sat gazing out at the sky,
And then, when her teacher, Miss Lubber, said, 'Lil?'
She'd shout out, **'Ahoy!'** in reply.

'Lil,' said Miss Lubber, 'stop daydreaming, please!
Remember you're here to learn facts!
Pirates aren't real! It's time now, I feel,
That you learned how a good schoolchild acts.'

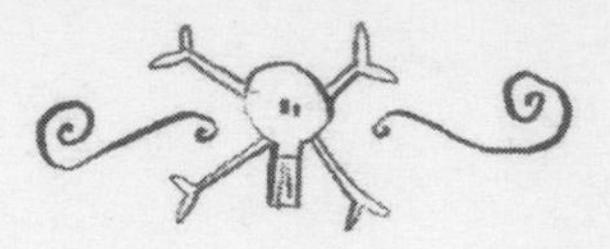

Lil hated to sit on her bum all day long.

Her school seemed most desperately dull.

But one day some paper appeared on her desk,

And on it . . .

the Sign of

the Skull!

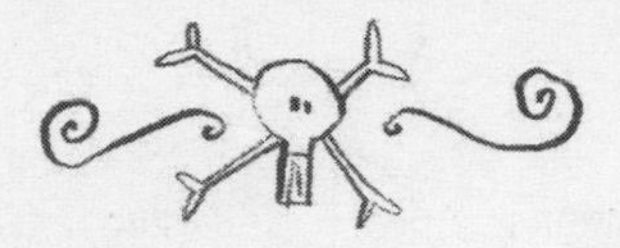

Lil shivered and shook as she thought to herself,

'We've trouble ahead, there's no doubt!

I know who drew *that* (oh, the rotten old rat!),

Yes, the terrible Stinkbeard's about!'

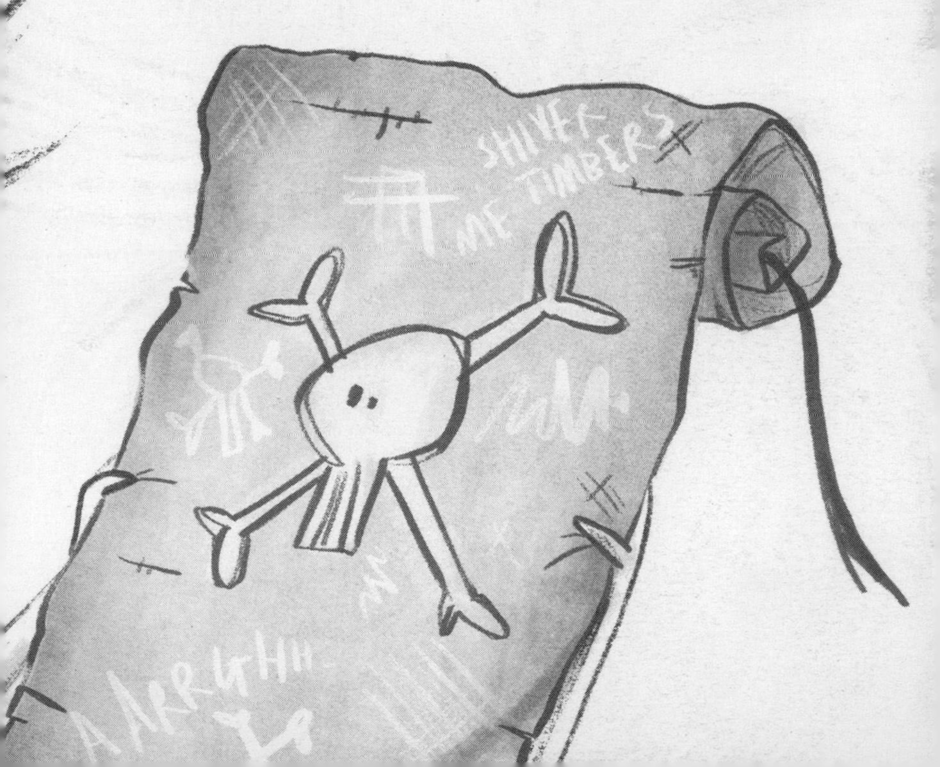

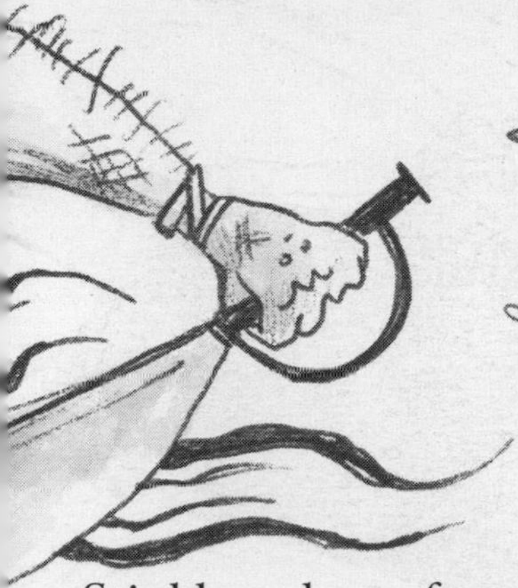

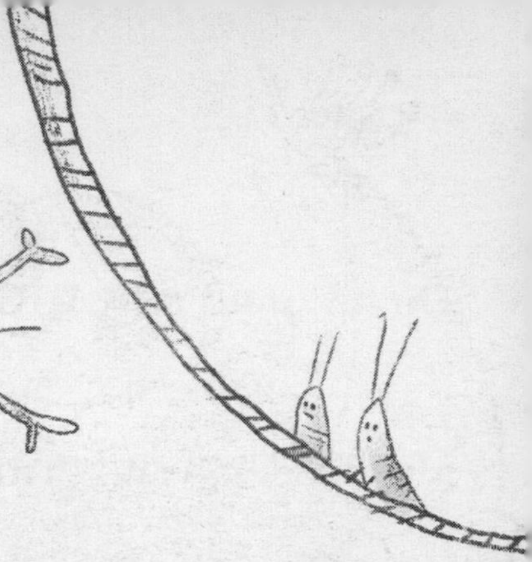

2

Stinkbeard was feared by all pirating folk;

He'd never, no NEVER, been nice.

He was flapping with fleas from his armpits to knees,

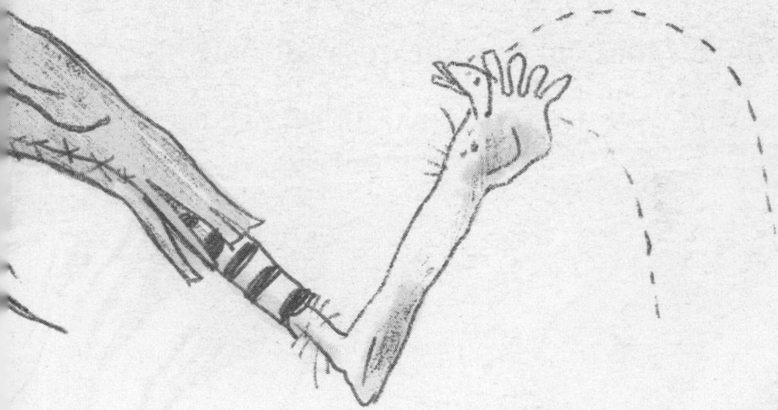

And even his toenails had lice.

On his beard grew mould, some thirty years old,

Encrusted with seaweedy slime.

He plundered and grabbed,

and he raided

and nabbed,

And all of his wealth came from crime.

Lil looked at the paper. 'That rascal!' she cried,

'What does old Stinkbeard want here?

Whatever he's plotting, that scoundrel needs stopping.

That much is perfectly clear.'

'Miss Lubber!' Lil shouted. 'Ahoy! Look outside!

There's a wicked old pirating guy!'

But her teacher said, 'Lil, just be quiet and sit still!

There *aren't* wicked pirates – don't lie!'

At playtime Miss Lubber said, 'Lil, stay inside!

Write "Children must all tell the truth".'

Lil whispered to Carrot, her trusty red parrot,

'Find Stinkbeard, and then be my sleuth.

‘That rotten old rat always talks to himself.

He mutters and mumbles all day.

So go and find out what he’s talking about.

We won’t let that brute get away!’

TICK
TOCK
TICK
TICK
TOCK
TOCK
TICK
TOC

3

Lil waited and waited for Carrot's return;

The minutes were ticking away.

Could Stinkbeard be found? Was he even around?

And what was he likely to say?

Stinkbeard was known for his dastardly deeds.

He'd even once burgled a bank!

What would he do? Snatch Year Two as his crew?

Or yell, 'Year One, walk the p l a n k'?

Suddenly Lil heard her parrot say, 'Pssst!'

But Miss Lubber came up, with a frown.

'This is no time for fun; there is work to be done!

Break-time is over!

Sit down!'

What could Lil do? She must go outside,

Yet Miss Lubber was sure to refuse.

She had to make haste. There was no time to waste,

Not one single moment to lose.

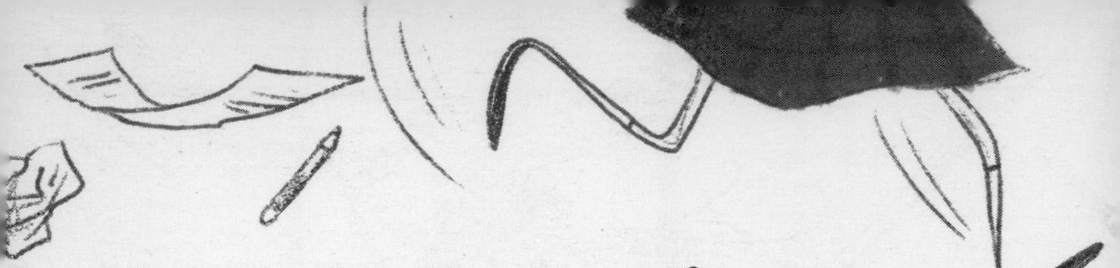

'Miss!' Lil yelled. 'There's a wasp in the room!

Or some kind of hornet or bee!

Look! Over here!

Over there! On that chair!

There's another one now – can't you see?'

The class started screaming and

screeching and shrieking

(One little boy even cried),

And as they all fled from imaginary bees . . .

Lil slipped unnoticed outside.

'Pieces of eight!' squawked Carrot the Parrot.

'Hurry up, Lil – we must dash!

That Stinkbeard is planning to kidnap Miss Lubber,

Then ask for a ransom in cash!'

'To the rescue!' Lil shouted to Carrot the Parrot.

'Now where's Stinkbeard lurking?' she said.

'We can't let that creature

get hold of my teacher!'

But Carrot just scratched at his head.

Lil searched

and she sniffed,

and she sniffed

and she searched.

'He's somewhere around, I can tell.

But just as I'd feared, he's quite disappeared!

Quickly now – follow that smell!'

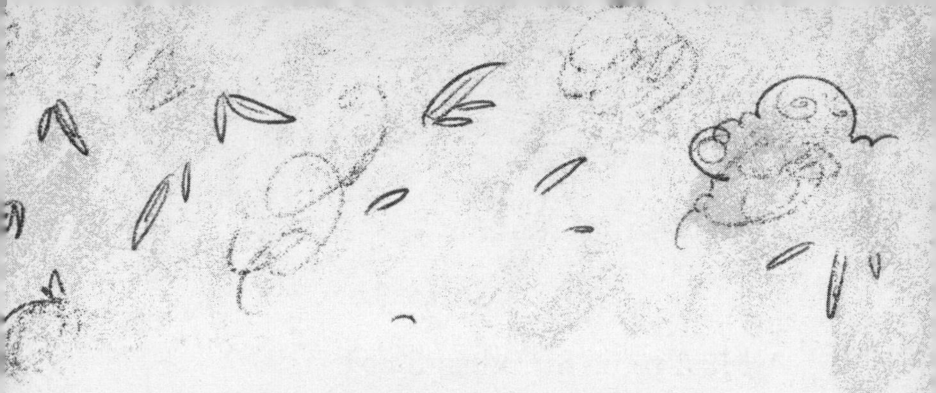

In all of the places that Stinkbeard had been,

A horrible **pong** filled the air.

Lil bravely went on, but it seemed he had gone;

That scoundrelly scum wasn't there!

But whose was that shadow

so sneakily snaking?

It had to be Stinkbeard at last!

'Now,' whispered Lil, 'I must get him, but how?

I'll have to be ever so fast!'

Lil grabbed at the ropes from some children

out skipping.

'Oi!' they all shouted. 'Don't snatch!'

But Lil said, 'I'll borrow them, just till tomorrow,

Right now, there's a pirate to catch!'

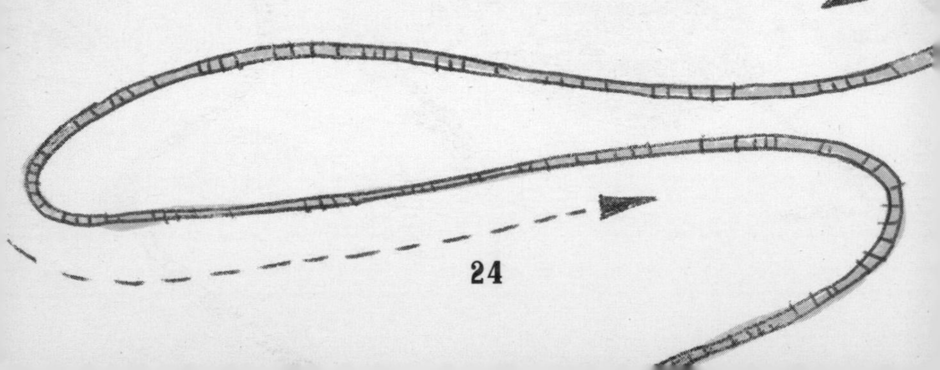

'Arrrrrrgh!' shouted Lil as she leaped in the air
And tied up old Stinkbeard with rope.
'You won't get away if you try for a day!
Don't struggle – you've not got a hope.'

But all of a sudden the man turned right round.

What horror! Oh, what a disaster!

It was not, as Lil thought, old Stinkbeard

she'd caught,

Instead she had got . . .

the Headmaster!

'Oops!' muttered Lil. 'Just a little mistake.

Really quite easily done.

But if you don't mind, I've a pirate to find,

So now, I'm afraid, I must . . . RUN!'

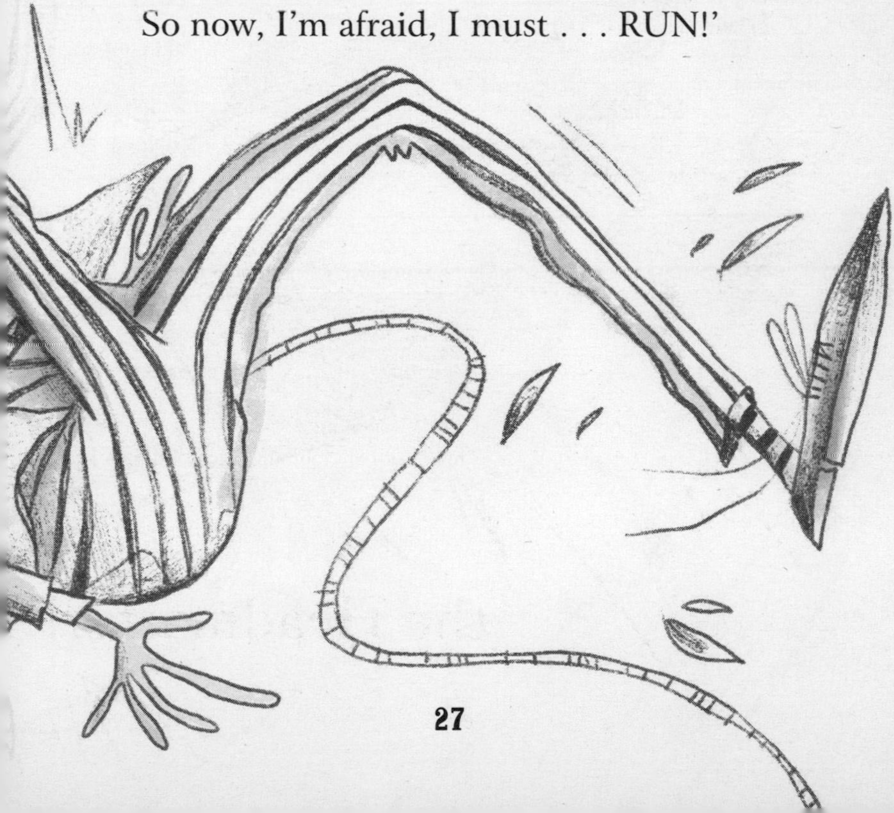

5

There was no time to think. Lil raced up a tree

As fast as she could, at the double.

The Headmaster was fuming, and furiously

BOOMING:

'Young Lil, you're in terrible trouble!'

But wait. What was that – up overhead?

Lil parted the leaves and she peered.

The *thing* was all bristly and grimy and gristly;

It wasn't a bird, but a . . .

. . . beard!

'Got you!' cried Lil. 'Don't you dare snatch

Miss Lubber,

You foul-breathed and frightful old

fiend!

And oh, by the way, I just thought I'd say

Your abominable beard should be

cleaned.'

Stinkbeard gave Lil the most gruesome great grin

As he narrowed his mean little eyes.

'A girlie? How cute! You'd be lovely as loot,

I will take you away as my prize!'

'Never!' Lil yelled. 'Get out of my school,

You vicious and villainous man!

You think that you'll snatch me?

Come on then – catch me!

Just try it and see if you can.'

With a cry of, 'Avast!' Lil leaped from the tree

(A trampoline stood right below).

She bounced in the air, and right then and there

Turned somersaults, three in a row.

Lil raced through the playground, she raced

through the school.

Stinkbeard was hot on her heels.

'The thing that I need,' Lil said, 'is more speed.

I know – I'll have to use . . .

wheels!'

The lunch cart was laden with food for school dinner;

With pizzas and salads and cakes.

Lil tore through the rooms.

How she zipped!

How she zoomed!

But then Carrot squawked,

'Help! There aren't brakes!'

With a crash and a smash and a clatter and clash,

The trolley went *wham!* in the wall.

All the shelves full of books,

all the coats on their hooks,

Everything started to fall.

Therc was nowhere to run,

there was nowhere to hide,

As Stinkbeard yelled, 'Got you, young creature!

Whatever you say, you won't get away.

And now, I will **kidnap** your teacher.'

6

‘Think of the ransom I’ll get,’ Stinkbeard said,

‘When Miss Lubber is tied to my mast!

She won’t get away till the Headmaster pays.

I’ll be wonderfully

wealthy

at last!

'You see?' Stinkbeard crowed, 'I'm as clever as ever!

Oh, poor little girl – I'm the winner!'

'Really?' Lil sneered. 'Oh you beastly old beard!'

And she pelted him hard with school dinner.

Pieces of pizza went *whoosh!* through the air,

There was ketchup all over the place.

Stinkbeard said, 'Help!' and he let out a yelp,

As some custard went *splat!* in his face.

Gravy oozed down from the top of his head,

Eggs went *ker-splot!* in his eyes.

'Just let me be!' Stinkbeard yelled, 'I can't see!

I'm covered in burgers and fries!'

‘Promise you won’t snatch Miss Lubber,’ said Lil,

‘You scurvy old scoundrelly scum!’

Then just as he fled, down Carrot sped

And bit Stinkbeard – peck-peck – on the bum.

‘Phew!’ said Lil. ‘Good riddance, at last.

Now I think that I might have a nap.’

But then she bent down, and she said, with a frown,

‘Oh look! Stinkbeard’s dropped this old map!

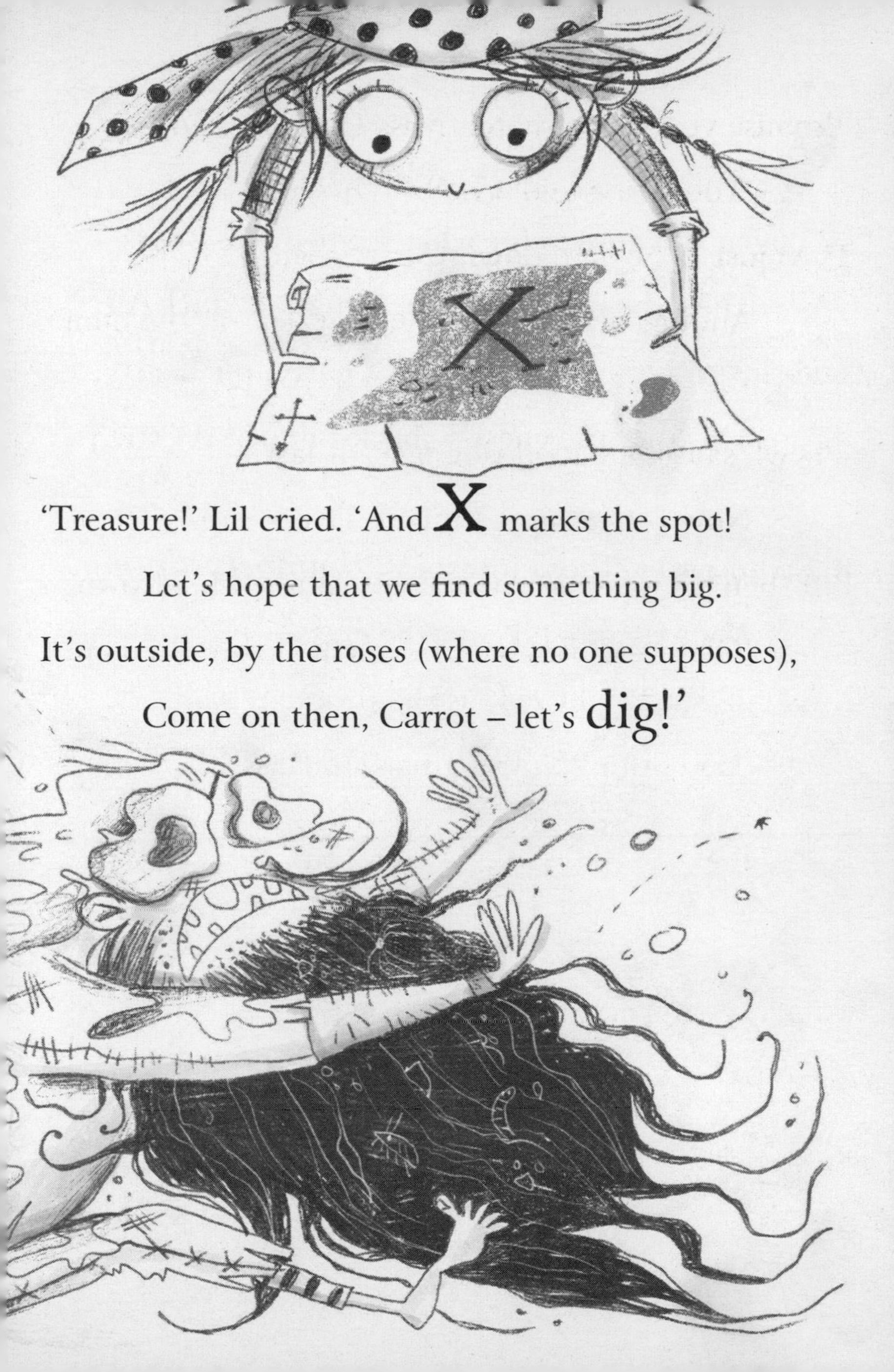

'Treasure!' Lil cried. 'And **X** marks the spot!

Let's hope that we find something big.

It's outside, by the roses (where no one supposes),

Come on then, Carrot – let's **dig!**'

Lil dug at the flowers for what seemed like hours,

Then she came to a barrel marked TREATS.

And she said to her parrot, 'Let's party, me hearty,

This treasure chest's chock-full of sweets!'

But whose were those footsteps, *thumpety-thump*,

Approaching Lil over the grass?

Miss Lubber! Bright red, as she furiously said,

'Detention! Now get back to class!'

'But I saved you,' cried Lil,

'from a fate worse than death!'

Miss Lubber said, 'No, you're just naughty.

Now sit over there and don't move from that chair.

And tell me, what's twenty

plus forty?'

'Huh!' muttered Lil as she stomped to her desk,
'Miss Lubber is really the worst!
If I wasn't so nice I might give some advice
And say she *deserved* to be cursed!

'But I am a pirate, a good sort of pirate,
And when there is someone to save,
Then I'll do what is right (if it takes me all night).
Yes, I'll always be **bold** and be **brave.**'

So Lil simply sat doing sums in her class,

And nobody, nobody knew

That Lil was a hero, a **swashbuckling** hero,

And all her adventures were **true**.

Croc Ahoy!

1

When Miss Lubber said,

'Class, it's your sports day today,'

Nobody, nobody guessed

That in matters of skill there was no one like Lil.

She was, in fact, simply . . .

THE BEST.

Yes, Lil was a pirate, a swashbuckling pirate,

Who'd spent half her life up a mast.

She could jump,

she could chase,

she could swim,

she could race,

And whatever she did, she did fast.

She could flee through the sea,

she could scale up a tree,

She could sail with the whales all day long.

She could throw, she could catch,

she could win any match,

She was bold, she was brave, she was strong.

So Lil cried, 'Let's go, with a yo, ho, ho!'

When her class all filed off to the park,

Though doing PE wasn't nearly as fun

As battling a

shadowy

shark.

'Now', said Miss Lubber, 'take care on the street.

Make sure that you hold a friend's hand.

Children, this way! Lil, do as I say!

And *why* are you covered in sand?

'Cross at the lights. Walk on the right.

Don't chatter!

Don't natter!

Don't talk!

And was that a child or a bird that I heard?

It sounded a bit like a squawk!'

They arrived at the park and Miss Lubber said,

'Kids, The mayor of the city is here!

She'll hand out each prize. Such a lovely surprise!'

The class gave a bored little cheer.

But Lil wasn't listening; she sat near the lake,

Dreaming of trophies she'd win,

When she saw in the grass near the rest of her class

A horrid and hideous grin.

'What a strange-looking puppy', Lil said to herself,

Then she suddenly shuddered in shock.

It wasn't a dog by the side of the log,

But a greedy and villainous . . .

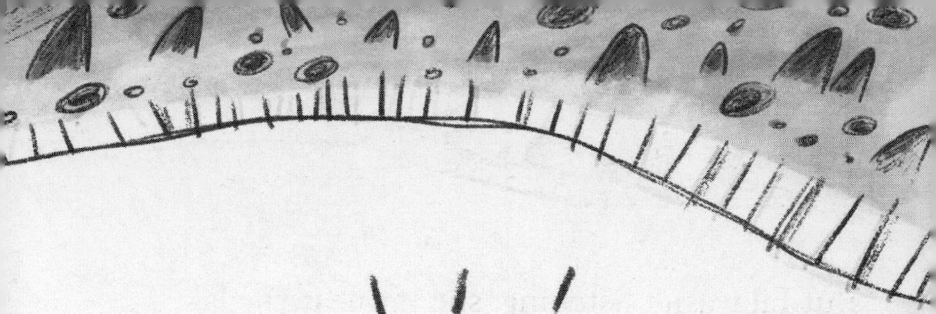

croc!

Its eyes were like glass, its teeth were like knives,

Its claws were all poised to attack.

And Lil said, 'I bet that's a foul pirate's pet!

Yes, that scurvy old Stinkbeard's

come back!'

2

Lil watched as the croc licked its horrible lips,

On the lookout for something to eat.

And Lil thought, 'It's wild! It will **guzzle** each child!

It will **gobble** them up from their feet!

'Those teeth will go *slash!*

They will slice!

They will mash!

They will grind all my friends to a pulp!

Then that croc will think,

"Yum! Little child in my tum!"

And will swallow them down in one gulp!

'Whatever old Stinkbeard is after this time,

It's clear that he wants us all chop-*ped*.

I'll discover his plan and then do what I can.

That crook and his **croc** must be stopped!'

But just as Lil thought, 'I will follow that croc!'

Miss Lubber yelled, 'Lil, over here!

The races will start and you're here to take part!

At once!

Is that perfectly

clear?

'So these are the rules: stay AWAY from the mud.

Do NOT climb the fences or walls.

Don't cheat. Be fair. And be nice to the mayor.

Now can you remember that all?'

'Maybe,' said Lil. Miss Lubber just frowned,

Saying, 'Come along, children, get set.

On your marks, get ready!

Breathe in!

Get steady!'

When *something* squawked,

Children ran.

Children stopped.

Children scratched at their heads.

The race was in full disarray.

'Nice work,' muttered Lil to Carrot the Parrot,

And silently slipped right away.

3

A climbing frame stood near the pond in the park,

Looking ever so scary and high.

But Lil thought, 'From there I can spy everywhere.

To climb that's as easy as pie.'

up,
and
up
Higher she rose, up,

To the uppermost place she could get.

And there she could see, through the leaves of a tree,

Stinkbeard, in talks with his pet.

'Aha!' chuckled Lil. 'It's clear from up here,

I can hear every whispery word.

I'll listen,' said Lil, keeping perfectly still,

And here's what she then overheard:

'Crockles, my precious, here is our plan:

We'll be brave!

We'll be **brutish** and **bold**!

Gobble those kids with a crunch for your lunch,

Then we'll steal all those trophies of gold.'

'Right, this is war!' spluttered Lil to herself.

'And now let the battle commence!
When Stinkbeard knows that I'm one of his foes
He will flee, if he has any sense!

'Carrot,' she whispered, 'prepare your attack,

And aim for that slimeball's bald head.

Lil said with a shout,

'I've got you, so tremble in dread!'

Carrot swooped down towards Stinkbeard and Croc,

Closer and closer he flew.

'And now meet your fate,' yelled Lil, 'I can't wait.

Carrot, release all the poo!

‘Stinkbeard, you vermin,’ Lil yelled in the breeze,

‘You rotten old rascally creature!

You’re nothing! You’re dust!’ Then the wind

gave a gust,

And the poo blew on top of . . .

Lil’s teacher!

4

'Come here **at once**,' bawled Miss Lubber to Lil,

As poo oozed in streams down her nose.

There was poo on her face and all over the place:

In her hair,

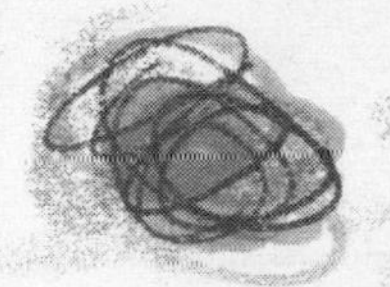

on her bag,

on her clothes!

'Lil,' she said, 'none of your stories this time.

You're in dreadful, yes DREADFUL, disgrace!

I made it quite clear that you couldn't play here.

Now of course you are banned from the race.'

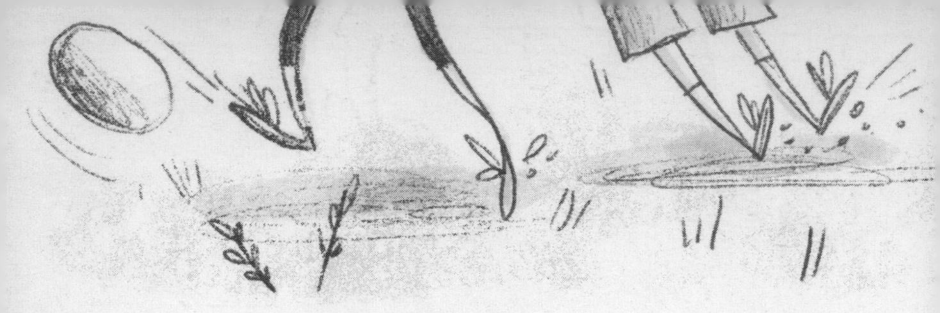

'Humph!' muttered Lil. 'She can say what she likes,

But I'll not be so easily beaten.

If I don't act, then I know for a fact

That my friends will be

chewed up

and eaten.'

Lil sat all alone as her friends ran around,

Some of them cheering and clapping.

But what was that noise? Not girls and not boys;

It sounded distinctly like . . .

. . . snapping!

What could Lil do? Where could she go?

She hadn't a moment to think!

There stood the croc!

Lil's heart beat *knock-knock*

As its eye gave a hideous wink.

'Feed it,' squawked Carrot. 'Then fill up its tum,

Before it finds kiddies to crunch.

It's dripping with drool!

It will eat the whole school!

But maybe it likes . . .

school packed lunch!'

Creeping and crawling, Lil looked for some food;

Her movements were silent and stealthy.

There on the grass was the lunch for her class,

All of it ever so healthy.

There was celery, lettuce and lumpy white cheese,
Tomatoes and brown bread with crusts.
The croc gulped them down,
gave a strange little frown . . .
Then spat them all out in disgust!

Lil looked around for some tastier food;
The mayor's lunch seemed toothsome enough,
With large sausage rolls, crisps in small bowls,
And biscuits and other such stuff.

'It's not really stealing,' Lil said to herself.

'The lives of small kids are at stake!

Croccy!' she said, as it reared its large head.

'Come over here – have some cake.'

The croc grinned with greed and ate it all up,

With a slibbery slobbery slurp.

Its belly was filled. It sat looking chilled,

Then it gave an enormous great . . .

BURP!

And just as Lil thought,

'Good, we're safe here at last!'

Miss Lubber said, 'What was that sound?'

And she saw, not a claw or a crocodile jaw,

But ALL of the mess on the ground.

'Oops!' muttered Lil. 'It's a bit of a tip,

But you always claim tidying's fun.

I'll leave it to you and the others to do.

And now, er, I think . . .

I must RUN!'

5

Faster than lightning Lil whizzed through the park.

Miss Lubber yelled, 'Oi, there, come back!'

With trees as trapezes Lil zipped

through the breezes,

And flew like a flash down each track.

She crashed through the bushes,

she leaped over flowers,

Cutting a path at a dash.

Then, not really knowing what way she was going,

Lil fell in the mud with a splash.

Lil was covered in ooze from her head to her shoes.

'Huh!' muttered Lil. 'Just my luck!'

But no one behind her was likely to find her

All coated in sludge and in muck.

'Phew!' muttered Lil, wiping mud from her mouth.

But what was that horrible growl?

And what was that stench,

over there,

by the bench?

It was Stinkbeard, still out on the prowl!

With a wild 'A-harrr!' Lil leaped from the mud,

Dripping with slippery slime.

'You stinker!

You plotter!

You scumbag!

You rotter!

Beware – I will get you this time!'

Stinkbeard went white. He gave a small yelp.

His knees started shaking in shock.

'A monster!' he cried. 'Oh, help! I must hide!'

And he fled from the park with his croc.

'Shiver me timbers – I've done it!' cheered Lil.

'Now I hope that he never comes back.'

Then Lil said, 'Oh dear! Now Miss Lubber is here!'

And she dived in a nearby sack.

6

Sports day was finally reaching an end,
With only one race left to go.
Who would come first? Who would be worst?
Who would be fast, and who slow?

The whistle went off. The children began
Jumping in sacks up the hill.
But whose was that sack at the front of the track?
Of course! Yes, the winner was . . .

Lil!

'What?' screeched Miss Lubber.

'That girl's a disgrace,

Who never behaves as she's told.

She's a naughty young child, she's totally **wild**.

Lil doesn't **deserve** to win gold.'

'I can see,' said the mayor,

'that she's covered in muck,

But I'm sure she was just having fun.

This girl was the best, she beat all the rest,

So she gets the prize.

Yes, she's won.'

'Oo-arrr!' whispered Lil to her trusty old parrot.

'It seems that I've got us some **booty**.

It's the best bit of bounty in all of the county,

Isn't it, Carrot, me beauty?'

Then Lil simply went back to school with her class,

And nobody, nobody knew

That Lil was a **hero**, a swashbuckling hero,

And all her adventures were **true**.

More fun from

ELLI WOOLLARD

For younger readers

For younger readers

And look out for

Coming soon!